FEB '96

WI

NATIVE AMERICAN WOMEN

THE JUNIOR LIBRARY OF
AMERICAN INDIANS

NATIVE AMERICAN WOMEN

Suzanne Clores

CHELSEA JUNIORS 🌿

a division of CHELSEA HOUSE PUBLISHERS

FRONTISPIECE: Paiute activist Sarah Winnemucca, photographed in 1885.

CHAPTER TITLE ORNAMENT: A drawing of a Navajo doll.

English-language words that are italicized in the text can be found in the glossary at the back of the book.

Chelsea House Publishers
EDITORIAL DIRECTOR Richard Rennert
EXECUTIVE MANAGING EDITOR Karyn Gullen Browne
COPY CHIEF Robin James
PICTURE EDITOR Adrian G. Allen
CREATIVE DIRECTOR Robert Mitchell
ART DIRECTOR Joan Ferrigno
PRODUCTION MANAGER Sallye Scott

The Junior Library of American Indians
SENIOR EDITOR Martin Schwabacher

Staff for NATIVE AMERICAN WOMEN
ASSISTANT EDITOR Catherine Iannone
EDITORIAL ASSISTANT Sydra Mallery
ASSISTANT DESIGNER Lydia Rivera
PICTURE RESEARCHER Villette Harris
COVER ILLUSTRATOR Shelly Pritchett

First Printing

1 3 5 7 9 8 6 4 2

Library of Congress Cataloging-in-Publication Data

Clores, Suzanne.
Native American women/ Suzanne Clores.
  p. cm. — (The Junior library of American Indians)
Includes index.
       0-7910-2479-2
       0-7910-2480-6 (pbk.)
1. Indian women—North America—History—Juvenile literature. 2. Indians of North America—History—Juvenile literature. [1. Indian women—History. 2. Indians of North America—History.] I. Title. II. Series.
E98.W8C56 1995   94-45258
305.48'897—dc20   CIP
                                                  AC

CONTENTS

This 1832 painting by
George Catlin depicts a
buffalo hunt, the primary
source of food for the
Teton Sioux.

Chapter 1

White Buffalo Woman

One summer long ago, the Sioux Indians were starving because their hunters could not find any *game*. Scouts were sent out every day, but they came back empty handed each time. One day, the scouts climbed a high hill in order to see far across the land. In the distance they saw a figure floating toward them.

The approaching figure was a beautiful young woman. She wore a white *buckskin* outfit that sparkled in the sun. It was decorated with a *sacred* design made with brightly colored porcupine quills. She carried a large sack and a fan of sage leaves. Her hair was blue-black and tied up at the side with buffalo skin. Her cheeks were dotted with red face paint. As she approached the scouts, they saw her dark eyes sparkling and knew that there was great power in them.

The two scouts stared at her. One was *awestruck* and did not move, but the other, disrespectfully, tried to touch her. At that moment, lightning struck the second scout and burned him to a black heap of bones.

The woman looked at the first scout and said, "Go and tell your people that I bring good and holy things from the buffalo nation. Tell them to prepare the medicine lodge and make things holy for my coming."

The young scout ran back to camp. He told the chief what the sacred woman had commanded. The people at camp quickly put up the medicine tepee and awaited the holy woman's arrival. Four days later, they saw a glimmer of the white buckskin dress from afar. Soon the woman arrived at the camp, carrying her bundle. The chief invited her inside the medicine lodge and watched her move around the tepee in the same circular motion as the sun. He told her gratefully, "Sister, we are glad you have come to instruct us."

The mysterious visitor showed the people how to build a sacred altar. Then she stood before the chief and took a pipe from her bundle. The people noticed that she grasped

Blackfoot women of 19th-century Montana tan a hide. The Blackfeet had a way of life similar to the Teton Sioux.

the stem of the pipe with her right hand, and with her left hand she grasped the bowl. This is how the Sioux have held their ceremonial pipes ever since.

The woman taught the people how to use the pipe. She told them that the rising smoke was the living breath of the great Grandfather Mystery (Wakan Tanka). Then she showed them the right way to pray, with the correct words and body motions.

"With this holy pipe," she said, "you will walk like a living prayer. Wakan Tanka smiles on us because now we are as one: earth, sky, all living things, the two-legged, the four-legged, the winged ones, the trees, the grasses. Together with the people, they are all related, one family. The pipe holds them all together."

The holy woman then spoke to the women of the tribe. She told them it was the work of their hands and the fruit of their bodies that kept the Sioux alive. "You are from the Mother Earth," she said. "What you do is as great as what the warriors do."

She gave the women the gifts of corn, wild turnip, and most importantly, pemmican. (Pemmican is meat that is dried over a fire and ground so that it can be stored for a long time. For tribes such as the Sioux who depended on hunting, pemmican was essential to their diet.) She taught the women how to build the hearth fire and how to cook food by dropping red hot stones into a buffalo sack full of water.

The woman then spoke to the children. "You are the coming generation. That is why you are the most important and precious ones. Someday you will hold this pipe and smoke it. Someday you will pray with it."

The sacred woman turned to face all the people and said, "I shall see you again," and she walked off in the direction from which she had come.

The people were watching her go when she suddenly stopped and dropped to the ground. She rolled over once and turned into a black buffalo. Then she rolled over again and became a brown one. The third time she became a red buffalo, and the fourth time she rolled over, she turned into a white female buffalo calf. The people were astonished: a white buffalo was the most sacred living thing one could ever encounter. The mysterious visitor came to be known as White Buffalo Woman.

As she disappeared over the horizon, tremendous herds of buffalo appeared in her place, allowing themselves to be killed for the people's survival. After White Buffalo Woman's visit, the buffalo furnished the Sioux with everything they needed—meat for food, skins for clothes and tepees, and bones for tools.

This story shows how highly women were respected among the Sioux. Although the Sioux placed great value on hunting and warfare, in which only men participated, they credited a woman with feeding and blessing the tribe, providing the people with everything they needed to survive.

Many other tribes have traditional stories in which women play important roles in creating and helping their people. The Cherokees believe that corn and beans sprang from the body of the first woman, Selu, also known as Corn Mother. According

The Iroquois Story of the Creation of the World

Long ago, before there were human beings, there were Sky People. In those days there was no sun. All light came from the white blossoms of the great tree that stood before the lodge of the Sky Chief. When the Sky Chief's young wife, Sky Woman, became pregnant, the troublesome Firedragon spread a rumor that Sky Chief was not the father of his wife's child. In a fit of anger and jealousy, Sky Chief uprooted the great tree and pushed his wife through the hole where the tree had stood.

Sky Woman fell toward the vast dark waters below. The birds, feeling sorry for her, gently caught her. The sea animals hurried to make a place for her. They plunged to the bottom of the water and brought up soil, which they placed on Turtle's back, forming the world. The light from the blossoms of the fallen tree shone through the hole where it had stood and became the sun. When Sky Woman landed, the world was ready for her, with grass and trees beginning to grow.

Sky Woman gave birth to a daughter, who eventually became the mother of twin boys—one good and one evil. The Evil Twin was in such a hurry to be born that he pushed through his mother's side, killing her. Sky Woman buried her daughter, and plants miraculously grew from her daughter's body—a cornstalk, a bean bush, and a squash vine. This was the origin of the Iroquois' most important crops.

to Iroquois legend, people were created by the descendants of a woman who fell from the sky. Sky Woman had one daughter, and when she died, corn, beans, and squash grew from her grave. These crops became the essential foods of the Iroquois. The Iroquois called them Our Supporters, or the Three Sisters.

These stories show the importance of Indian women to the survival of their tribes. Standing Bear, a leader of the Ponca Indians, expressed his appreciation for women when he said that his mother, "in her humble way, helped to make the history of her race. For it is the mothers, not her warriors, who create a people and guide her destiny." ◣

William Penn's Treaty with the
Indians, *painted in 1771, depicts*
a meeting between Penn, the founder
of Pennsylvania, and male members
of the Delaware, Susquehannock,
and Shawnee tribes.

Chapter 2

"Where Are Your Women?"

Most of the stories that early white explorers and settlers recorded about Native Americans failed to mention women. This is partially because the Europeans glorified the activities of men, especially hunting and warfare, and did not recognize the contributions of women. Another reason is that white men had little respect for women. When they came into contact with Native Americans, they refused to meet with women, even though women played an important role in tribal government, religion, and trade.

There is a well-known story about a group of Cherokee Indians who met with British representatives in the 18th century.

15

Outacitty, the leader of the Cherokee group, was surprised that all the British representatives were men. The Cherokees never made important decisions without consulting the women of the tribe. Outacitty's first words to the British were: "Where are your women?" But the British did not value the opinions of women and did not want them to be present at important meetings.

Many tribes, including the Iroquois, the Mohegans, the Chickasaws, the Seminoles, the Pawnees, the Navajos, the Hopis, and the Zunis, are matrilineal. This means that a child's lineage, or line of relatives, is traced through his mother, unlike European societies, in which children take the last name of their father.

In some Indian societies, such as the Cherokee and the Iroquois, women created the community government. When it came to decision making, women were responsible for representing children's interests as well as their own. Their opinions carried a lot of weight because they were speaking for the good of many.

The most *influential* women of the tribe were the clan mothers. A clan is a type of extended family in which all members share a common ancestor. The clan mother was usually the oldest female member. Clan mothers *nominated* chiefs and subchiefs and advised them in times of war. In Iroquois societies, the clan mother had the power to forbid the men from going on the warpath. The chiefs often used this power to their benefit when they did not want to go to war with another tribe. They would simply tell the enemy tribe, "We cannot war with you. Our clan mother forbids it."

Sarah Winnemucca, a Paiute Indian from Nevada, described the participation of women in Paiute society in her 1883 autobiography, *Life Among the Piutes:*

> The women know as much as the men do, and their advice is often asked. . . . The council-tent is our Congress, and anybody can speak who has anything to say, women and all. They are always interested in what their husbands are doing and thinking about. And they take some part even in the wars. They are always near at hand when fighting is going on, ready to snatch up their husbands and carry them off if wounded or killed. . . . If women could go into your Congress, I think justice would soon be done to the Indians.

Native American women were highly respected because their contributions were vital to the survival of their tribes. Men and women possessed different skills, and they realized that they needed each other's abilities to survive. The Blackfoot Indians tell a story about this relationship.

According to the legend, Old Man created the world, and he made men and women live apart. Old Man eventually realized that

they would be happier living together, so he went to visit the women. When he saw the women's village, he said, "What a good life they're having! They have fine tepees made of tanned buffalo *hide*, while we men have only brush shelters of raw, stinking green hides to cover us. And look what fine clothes they wear, while we have to go around with a few pelts around our loins! I made a big mistake putting the women so far away from us."

Old Man went back to his village to tell the men what he had seen. The chief of the women's village discovered Old Man's footprints and sent a young woman to follow them. The woman saw the men's village and

Omaha Indian women grind corn in front of an earth lodge. This type of house was built by the women of several Plains tribes.

rushed back to her village to tell the women what she had seen: "There's a camp over there with human beings living in it. They seem different from us, taller and stronger. Oh, sisters, these beings live very well, better than us. They have a thing shooting sharp sticks, and with these they kill many kinds of game—food that we don't have. They are never hungry."

The men and women agreed that they would be happier living together. The story concludes: "Then the women moved in with the men. They brought all their things, all their skills to the men's village. Then the women quilled and *tanned* for the men. Then the men hunted for the women. Then there was love. Then there was happiness. Then there was marriage. Then there were children."

Although men and women in each tribe specialized in different skills, the distinction between men's work and women's work was not always clear. Pueblo Indian men assisted their wives with their domestic duties and made clothing and blankets. Among the Crow Indians, some men dressed and lived as women, and some women went to war. In other tribes, there are numerous stories about women rushing onto the battlefield to protect or substitute for their fallen husbands and brothers. In many instances, they

Minnie Hollow Wood, a Sioux shown here in 1927, earned the right to wear a warbonnet after taking part in combat against the U.S. cavalry.

were later given the privilege of fighting, or they earned war titles that gave them the honor of singing and dancing during warriors' rituals.

One woman warrior has become a legend among the Blackfoot Indians. She began life with the name Brown Weasel Woman. As a child, she asked her father, a well-known warrior, to teach her to hunt. The other tribe members did not think that she should learn a man's skill, but her father made her a bow and arrows so that she could practice shooting. Soon he brought her on buffalo hunts, and she became a skilled hunter.

During one of these hunts, the Blackfoot hunters were attacked by an enemy tribe. As the hunters fled their attackers, the horse of Brown Weasel Woman's father was shot. Brown Weasel Woman knew that without his horse her father would be killed, so she turned around, braving the enemy, and rescued her father. Facing an enemy's attack to rescue someone stranded on foot was one of the bravest acts a Blackfoot warrior could perform.

Brown Weasel Woman continued to prove her bravery and skill in war. The chief honored her by giving her the name Running Eagle, which had belonged to some of the tribe's great warriors. She was also invited to join a society of young warriors. Thereafter, Running Eagle served as the leader of war parties, and many men were eager to follow her into battle.

Running Eagle is known as an unusual woman because she took the warpath, but there were many other strong, brave women whose stories will never be known. These are the women who built the foundations of Indian societies through traditional women's work. ▲

Women's Work

The story of Old Man illustrates the roles of men and women among the Indians of the Great Plains. The Plains Indians hunted buffalo to feed their tribes. But many other tribes, especially those who lived east of the Mississippi River and in the Southwest, relied on farming.

In the eastern tribes, women were responsible for farming. Men did most of the heaviest work, such as clearing forestland to make new fields, but women planted seeds, tended the growing plants, and harvested the crops. They also made gardening tools from wood, flint, tortoise shells, and the bones of large animals. The most important crops were corn, beans, and squash. Some tribes also grew potatoes, peanuts, peppers, tomatoes, sunflowers, tobacco, and plants from which medicines and dyes were made.

Women in these tribes earned respect for providing the community with its most important source of food. In 1788, an Iroquois named Domine Pater gave a speech on the importance of women in Iroquois society. Governor George Clinton of New York was so impressed by the speech that he had Pater's words written down: "Our ancestors considered it a great offence to reject the counsels of their women. . . . They were esteemed the mistresses of the soil (as they attended to the labours of *agriculture*). Who, said they, bring us into being? Who cultivates our land, kindles our fires (or administers food to the call of the hungry), but our women?"

Women also helped feed their communities by taking part in ceremonies that were believed to bring success in farming, hunting, or fishing. The Pueblos, for example, held a ceremony to ensure a successful hunt. It involved a group of men imitating deer, but the central figure in the ritual was a woman. *Anthropologist* Ruth Underhill described this ritual: "In their midst was a beautiful Pueblo woman with long black hair, in all the regalia of white boots and *embroidered* manta. She

A Hidatsa woman tends her cornfield with a hoe made of bone.

was their owner, the Mother of Game. But she was also Earth Mother, the source of all live things including men. She led the animals where they would be good targets for hunters, and, one by one, they were symbolically killed."

The Hidatsas, who lived in what is now North Dakota, were primarily farmers, but they also hunted buffalo. Two women's organizations performed ceremonies to bring the Hidatsas an abundance of food. The rituals of the Goose Society brought about a plentiful corn harvest. The White Buffalo Cow Society performed ceremonies to attract buffalo herds.

The participation of women in hunting rituals was important to their status in the tribe. Since hunting was a male activity, men received the honor of supplying meat to the community. By taking part in these ceremonies, women shared in the responsibility and rewards of the hunt.

Women of all tribes were skilled at preserving and preparing food. Corn was dried and ground into cornmeal, which was used to make soup or bread. Fresh corn could be boiled, roasted, baked, or fried to make a wide assortment of dishes. Women also had an understanding of nutrition. They knew that people must eat a variety of foods in order to maintain good health.

Wild plants were essential in providing this variety. Women gathered nuts, seeds, berries, roots, and herbs. Wild plant foods were especially important to tribes that did not grow food, such as the buffalo hunters of the Great Plains and the tribes of the northern Pacific Coast who primarily ate seafood.

Certain foods could not be eaten in their natural state. Women possessed a wealth of knowledge about preparing these plants to be eaten. For example, acorns were a dietary staple of many tribes in California, such as the Chumash. Acorns, however, contain an acid that makes them extremely bitter. Women learned to remove the acid by grinding the acorns into flour and pouring hot water through it several times. This flour was later mixed with water to make mush, or it was baked into cakes which were flavored with spices, meats, and berries.

Among the Plains Indians, women's work centered on preparing the buffalo and other game that the hunters brought home. The Great Plains is the expanse of flat land east of the Rocky Mountains. It stretches south to Texas and as far north as the Saskatchewan River in Canada. Some well-known Plains tribes include the Blackfeet, the Teton Sioux, the Cheyennes, the Arapahos, the Comanches, and the Kiowas.

As depicted in the story of White Buffalo Woman, these tribes depended on the buffalo to provide most of what they needed to survive. Because men were the primary suppliers of game, they had a more central role in hunting tribes than in those tribes that practiced agriculture. But women were respected for their ability to make food, clothing, shelter, and tools from the buffalo.

Women butchered the buffalo and cut the meat into thin strips that were hung over a

fire to dry. Drying the meat kept it from spoiling, so it could be stored to feed the tribe between hunting seasons. This dried meat could also be ground to produce pemmican, which could be stored even longer.

Maria Martinez, shown here with her husband, Julian, around 1940, helped revive interest in Pueblo pottery.

Buffalo were so valuable to the Plains tribes that the Indians developed uses for every part of the body. The meat and organs were eaten. Blood and fat were used to make soup and pudding. Sinew—the strong stringy tissue that attaches muscle to bones—was used as thread in sewing. Tools were made from bones. Spoons and small bowls were carved from the horns. The stomachs were dried and used to carry water and to store small objects such as beads and dried foods. The hair was spun into yarn that was woven to make blankets or braided to make rope. The skins were turned into clothing, tepee covers, moccasins, blankets, bags, shields, and countless other items.

The Plains Indians did not live in permanent villages. They were always moving and setting up new camps so they could be near the buffalo herds. This is why they lived in tepees—they needed homes that could easily be moved.

Tepees were built with about 20 poles that were each 25 feet long. Men cut the poles, but women constructed the tepees. The poles were stuck into the ground to form a circle about 15 feet across. The tops of the poles were tied together to make a cone shape. To make the cover, about 15 buffalo hides were sewn together to form a large semicircle. This was wrapped around the frame of poles and held in place with wooden pins. An opening was left in the top to allow smoke to escape. When the tribe had to move, the tepee could easily be taken down, carried to the next camp, and set up again.

Tribes that relied on farming or fishing usually lived in permanent villages. In most of these tribes, men built the houses, but there were a few exceptions. Some tribes in the eastern Plains hunted buffalo but also grew crops. The women of these tribes built earth lodges—houses made of wooden poles covered with packed soil or grass. Among the Pueblos and Navajos of the Southwest, men and women shared the work of building houses.

Clothing was usually made by women. Most tribes used animal skins, especially deerskins, to make garments. In the northern Plains, for example, women dressed in deerskin skirts and long-sleeved cloaks. In colder weather, they wore leggings under their skirts and ponchos over their shoulders.

Women in warmer climates made clothing from plant products. An early Spanish explorer who visited the coast of Texas reported that in addition to wearing deerskin, women wove skirts of Spanish moss. Spanish moss is a dry, grayish green plant that hangs from the branches of trees. Among some tribes of the Southeast, women wove clothing from grass or the inner bark of trees. The Pueblos were expert weavers of cotton cloth. Pueblo women's dresses were rectangular pieces of cloth that were wrapped

A Navajo woman
weaves a blanket.

under the left arm, tied over the right shoulder, and held in place by a cotton belt.

The creative talent of Native American women was apparent in the *adornment* of their clothes. One extraordinary artform was embroidering with porcupine quills. Quills could be dyed bright colors or used in their natural state. Women soaked the quills in their mouths to make them soft and then sewed them onto leather to form designs. Quill work required a great deal of patience and attention to detail. When sewn carefully, the quills formed a smooth, glossy surface.

The dyes used to color quills, leather, and basketry were made from natural materials. Tree bark, grass, berries, flowers, and many other plant products were used. Certain minerals found in rocks or soil produced magnificent colors.

Clothing was often decorated with beads made of shells, copper, stone, pottery, seeds, nuts, animal bone, or teeth. Although men produced most beads, women sewed the beads onto garments to make designs. After the arrival of white men in the Americas, European beads became popular ornaments.

Women made pottery in many parts of the present-day United States, but in the Southwest they turned it into an artform. A member of a Spanish expedition that reached the Southwest in 1581 wrote that Pueblo women produced pots "so excellent and delicate" that they "equal, and even surpass, the pottery made in Portugal."

Long before Native American women learned to make pottery, they had mastered the art of basket weaving. Baskets were made of various plant fibers, depending on what grew in a tribe's territory. Typical materials were grass, reeds, thin strips of wood, and the inner bark of trees. Women used fibers of different colors to weave designs into the baskets. Many tribes wove baskets so tightly that they could hold water. Food could be cooked in these baskets by adding heated rocks to boil the water. Baskets were also used to store and carry food and possessions.

Women played a key role in providing food, clothing, and shelter in Native American societies, and their opinions weighed heavily in tribal decisions. The arrival of Europeans in North America in the 16th century, however, caused upheavals that drastically changed the way of life of all American Indians. Among these changes were dramatic shifts in the roles and status of Native American women. ▲

*The Motokiks, members
of a Blackfoot women's
society, build their
meeting lodge during
a Sun Dance in 1891.*

Chapter 4

Europeans in America

Only a few decades after Christopher Columbus landed on the North American continent, European traders and explorers began arriving in the area of what would eventually become the United States. Some Native Americans benefited from their early contacts with Europeans. Such tribes as the Algonquins, the Hurons, and the Iroquois grew wealthy trading furs to the newcomers. But the presence of Europeans quickly began to take its toll on the native population.

Many Native Americans died from diseases that were brought over from Europe. Smallpox and measles had never existed in the Americas, so the Indians' bodies were not able to resist the diseases. *Epidemics* spread across the land, killing thousands of people and devastating communities. When white settlers began taking Indian land, many more Indians were killed while defending their territory, and tribes were forced to leave their traditional homelands.

Europeans disrupted the lives of all Native Americans, but Indian women often suffered the added trauma of being separated from their people. White traders and explorers raided villages, taking women captive. Native Americans had a tradition of capturing women from enemy tribes, but these women were treated with respect. They were adopted by families or married to someone in the tribe. They were considered tribe members, not prisoners.

An example of the way Native Americans treated captive women is the story of Mary Jemison, a white woman who was captured in 1758, at the age of 15, from her parents' farm in Pennsylvania. Jemison went to live with the Senecas—one of the five Iroquois tribes—and was adopted by two women who had lost a brother. She said that the women treated her as a sister, "the same as though I had been born of their mother." After Jemison had lived with them for five years, a Seneca chief wanted to send

Amelia Douglas was a mixed-blood who married a white fur trader. With her knowledge of Carrier Indian customs, she enabled her husband to survive on the Canadian frontier.

her back to her parents, but she would not leave her new Seneca family. Jemison married twice and had eight children. She remained with the Senecas until her death in 1833.

Native American women who were captured by white men were treated like ser-

vants. They were removed from tribal life, where they had been surrounded by friends and family. White men captured Indian women because few white women were willing to live in frontier areas. These men wanted female companionship, even if the women had to be forced into it. They also felt safer in Indian territory in the company of a woman from the area. She could provide food and shelter and act as an interpreter when dealing with local tribes.

Black Plume, a Black-foot Indian, and his two wives in 1892. Christians believed that women suffered under polygamy, but one of Black Plume's sons recalled that his father and mothers got along well.

One of these women earned a place in history for her valuable guidance. Sacagawea was a Shoshone Indian from present-day Idaho. As a child she was captured by Hidatsa Indians. They sold her to Toussaint Charbonneau, a Canadian trapper who became her husband. In 1804, Charbonneau was hired as a guide by Meriwether Lewis and William Clark. Lewis and Clark had been sent by President Thomas Jefferson to lead an expedition from St. Louis, Missouri, to the Pacific Ocean. Sacagawea and her newborn baby joined the expedition.

Although Sacagawea had not been in Shoshone territory since her childhood, she remembered the region well enough to lead the expedition through it. She served as an interpreter between the travelers and the many Native Americans encountered along the journey, and she helped the men survive by teaching them to find *edible* plants and medicinal herbs and by making buckskin clothing and moccasins. Lewis and Clark became famous for the success of their expedition, and they praised Sacagawea for her courage and resourcefulness.

Some Indian women married white men by choice, but these marriages stripped the women of the rights they had had in their tribes. In matrilineal societies, women owned land and controlled the profits made from it. They also had authority over their children. When a couple divorced in these tribes, the wife kept her land, home, and children.

Women who married white men expected to have these same rights, but as the wives of white men, they became subject to white men's laws. In white society, husbands took control of their wives' property. Many men married Indian women solely to get their land. These women were not free to divorce, as they had been in their own society. But, if a white man abandoned his Indian wife, she was left with nothing. He had the rights to all of her property as well as their children.

Women who remained with their tribes lost much of their status owing to the influence of white settlers and *missionaries*. Whites felt that Indians would be less of a threat if they lived like European Americans. In the 1820s, the U.S. government instituted its "civilization" policy. Some tribes, such as the Cherokees in Georgia, were told that they would be able to keep their land if they gave up their traditional ways and acted like whites.

During this time there was an influential Cherokee woman named Nanyehi. After demonstrating great leadership during a war against the Creek Indians, she was made governor of the Women's Council and given

continued on page 49

MODERN VISIONS

The artwork of modern Indian women expresses the many ways in which their history affects their lives in the modern world. On the following pages are works by eight Native American women whose art has been exhibited at the American Indian Community House Gallery/Museum, an Indian-owned gallery in New York City. These artists blend the past and the present by combining ancient designs with new images. Symbols that hold traditional meaning are used to convey the experiences and the hopes of modern Indians. These artists both commemorate past events and comment on modern life, often using techniques that were borrowed from other cultures. Many of these artworks convey the influence of traditional spiritual beliefs in the lives of Native Americans today.

Untitled, from series Coming into Power, *hand-tinted/hand-painted black-and-white photograph, by Wolf Clan Cherokee artist Shan Goshorn.*

My People Are Sacred, *acrylic/oil/collage on paper, 1991, by Jane Ash Poitras, a Cree from Fort Chipewyan, Alberta, Canada. This work commemorates the Battle of Wounded Knee and the OKA incident in Canada. The shields at the bottom represent the supernatural powers that warriors took with them into battle. These powers could be transferred by the shaman to other members of the tribe, such as children. "Indians today are wounded warriors," says the artist. "They must fight to recapture their spirit and balance."*

Wounded OKA, *acrylic/ oil/collage on paper, 1990, by Jane Ash Poitras. In the OKA incident, the construction of a golf course threatened sacred Mohawk land, but the Indians won their case in court.*

Resurrecting Fossil Fish, *acrylic on canvas, 1987, by Karen Coronado, a Lumbee from North Carolina. This piece represents an attempt to recapture the sensibilities of a lost heritage.*

Cedar Woman Spirit, *acrylic paint/paper, hand-made from cedar/silk background, 1988.*

Killer Whale Child, *acrylic paint/paper, handmade from cedar/silk background, 1988.*

As a small child in Petersburg, Alaska, Tlingit artist Edna Jackson learned from her mother how to make playthings out of objects collected on beaches and in the woods. Influenced by these early experiences, she makes use of natural materials, as well as paper made from bark and grasses, in her art today.

44

Red Bear Mask, *rope/wood metallic yarn/beads/ribbon/feathers/nickelsilver, 1987,* by Gail Tremblay, an Onondaga. By unifying materials that have different textures, Tremblay hopes to explore that which makes "the human spirit dance."

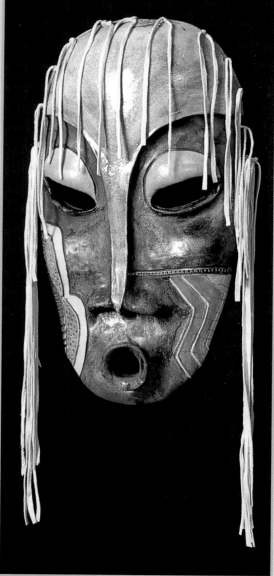

Pheasant Woman, *Raku/leather, 1988,* by Lillian Pitt, a Yakima from Warm Springs, Oregon. After firing her masks using Raku—a reduction process developed in 16th-century Japan—Pitt smolders them in beds of corn husks or grass and dresses them with feathers or buckskin fringe. Her work, she says, allows her to express how she feels about the earth.

The imagery in her art, Linda Lomahaftewa says, "comes from being Hopi and remembering shapes and colors from ceremonies and the landscape. I associate a special power and respect, a sacredness, with these colors and shapes, and this carries over into my own work."

Fragments of a Rainbow, *acrylic and rice paper on linen, 1988.*

Blue Cloud Maiden, *mono-type with oil pastel, 1989.*

In this monoprint, entitled The Female City Sky, by Santa Clara Pueblo/Navajo artist Beverly R. Singer, a buffalo leaps across sky-scrapers and a muddy river, demonstrating the persevering spirit of Indian women in urban settings. Like the buffalo, says Singer, women are a reservoir of freedom and strength. In the Pueblo tradition, Buffalo women dance every winter and spring to restore life-giving energy to their tribe.

Because Indian art is often thought of as having no ties to present life or to non-Indians, photography is critical to Shan Goshorn's work. "I want the viewer to realize that my subjects are . . . part of today. We are a contemporary people with strong roots in a traditional world."

Harmony for Our Seventh Generation, *hand-tinted black-and-white photocollage.*

Weaving in the Night, *hand-tinted/hand-painted black-and-white photograph.*

continued from page 40

the title Beloved Woman of the Cherokees. Many of her tribe members feared the whites and wanted to drive them out of their territory. Nanyehi, however, thought that it was necessary to befriend the whites. As the representative of the women, Nanyehi was able to prevent her tribe from going to war. For many years, she worked to maintain friendly relations between the Cherokees and the United States.

However, one of the requirements of the "civilization" policy was that women be excluded from tribal governments. Before 1920, American women did not have the right to vote in the United States. The U.S. government did not want Indian women to have political power either. In an attempt to satisfy the U.S. government, the Cherokees adopted a constitution based on that of the United States. It established a new form of government in which women had no voice. The Women's Council was dissolved and Nanyehi lost her political power.

The Cherokees began to live like white settlers. They learned to speak and read English, and they sent their children to mission schools. Many grew wealthy from farming or business and built elegant houses. Some even owned slaves. Despite the Cherokees' attempts to satisfy white Americans by

changing their way of life, the U.S. government broke its promise and forced them off their land. In 1838, the Cherokee Nation was forced to move to Indian Territory—present-day Oklahoma, Kansas, and Nebraska.

Throughout the 19th century, Native Americans were forced to give up their land and move to reservations. A reservation is a piece of land set aside for Indians. With the Indians confined to reservations, it was easier for the government to make them change their ways.

The U.S. government believed that Native Americans could be "civilized" only if they adopted the lifestyle of white farmers. Native American men had to give up hunting and settle down on farms. Land would be owned by men, and men would work the fields. Most whites believed that relieving women of their farming work would make their lives easier. But actually it robbed women of their power.

Women's agricultural work had empowered them because they could control the products of their labor. In agricultural tribes such as the Iroquois and the Hidatsas, women controlled the trade of corn and other crops. A government agent working in the Great Plains in the 1850s reported that "though the women perform all this labor, they are compensated by having their full

Anna Dawson, shown here with her mother in 1878, was an Arikara Indian who began studying at the Hampton Institute in Virginia at the age of 10. After graduating in 1885 and working as a teacher in the East, Anna returned to North Dakota to work among her people.

share of the profits." According to Mary Jemison, Iroquois women had more enjoyable lives than most American farm women. She said that their tasks were "probably not harder than that of white women . . . and their cares certainly are not half as numerous . . . we planted, tended, and harvested our corn, and generally had all our children with us; but had no master to oversee or drive us, so that we could work as leisurely as we pleased."

Plains Indians who had been buffalo hunters had to cope with even greater changes. They were not able to hunt on reservations. Men had traditionally attained honor through hunting and warfare. Now these activities were no longer part of their lives. Women had been able to gain status by excelling in tanning and quilling. Without the buffalo, however, these skills became useless.

The U.S. government further weakened women's roles in tribal *culture* by banning traditional ceremonies, songs, and dances. Women who had been central to their tribe's rituals lost their important roles in the community. One major ceremony that was banned was the Sun Dance—the most sacred ritual of the Plains Indians.

In the legends of the Plains Indians, the sun was the creator of the earth and everything living on it. At the Sun Dance, people *fasted* and made personal sacrifices to give thanks to the sun. Each tribe had its own variation of the ceremony. Among the Blackfeet, the Sun Dance was sponsored by a well-respected woman who had been granted a favor by the sun and wished to express her thanks. This woman was called Sacred Woman of the Dance, and she was treated respectfully by every member of the tribe during the four-day ceremony. In addition, a society of women called the Motokiks held their own meetings and ceremonies during the Sun Dance. When the Sun Dance and other ceremonies were banned, these women lost their special place in Blackfoot society.

After prohibiting Native Americans from practicing their religions, the U.S. government sent missionaries to the reservations to convert the Indians to Christianity. These missionaries urged the Indians to abandon some of their traditional ways of living. One practice that the missionaries found offensive was polygamy—the marriage of one man to two or more women. Christians thought that women would be happier if they did not have to share a husband. But polygamy had advantages for Native American women. In tribes that were often at war, many young men died in battle. These tribes usually had more women than men. Women

needed husbands to hunt for them, and without polygamy, many women would have been left unmarried.

Beverly Hungry Wolf, author of *The Ways of My Grandmothers*, states that some Blackfoot men had six or seven wives. In such large families, women often felt lonely, and many fell in love with other men. But in other cases, women were happy to share a husband. Often a woman would ask her husband to marry her sister. In this way, both sisters had a husband to provide them with meat and skins, and both could have children. They also had each other's com-

Students at the Cherokee Indian Seminary in 1889. Such schools separated Native Americans from their culture and taught them to fit into white society.

panionship and assistance with work. When Christians insisted that each man have one wife, the large families that were the backbone of tribal life were broken apart.

The government concentrated its *assimilation* efforts on young Native Americans. Children were taken away from their families and sent to boarding schools. These children did not have a chance to learn their tribal customs and history. They were taught to speak English, and many forgot their native language. Helen Sekaquaptewa, a Hopi woman, lived through the terrifying experience of being separated from her family and taken to school. She describes it in her 1906 autobiography, *Me and Mine.*

> We were now loaded into wagons hired from and driven by our enemies. . . . We were taken to the schoolhouse . . . into the big dormitory, lighted with electricity. . . . I had never seen so much light at night. . . . Evenings we would gather . . . and cry softly so the matron would not hear and scold or spank us. . . . I can still hear the plaintive little voices saying, "I want to go home. I want my mother." We didn't understand a word of English and didn't know what to say or do.

Schooling was intended to separate Indian children from their culture and teach them to live in white America. When they grew up, however, many women used their education to fight against the government policies that were destroying their culture. ▲

Members of the National Council of American Indians visit the studio of Ulric Dunbar to view his statue of Sitting Bull. Gertrude Bonnin, the president of the council, stands beside the statue.

Chapter 5

Building the Future

In the late 19th century, Native Americans began using their education to save the heritage that the schools intended to destroy. One early reformer was Sarah Winnemucca, an educated Paiute Indian who served as a scout and interpreter for the U.S. Army. The Paiutes had once controlled a vast territory in Nevada. By the late 19th century, most of their land had been taken, and they were living in poverty. Winnemucca's public life began in 1879, when she and a group of Paiutes were forced onto a reservation in Washington State. The conditions were so poor that many Paiutes died during the harsh winter.

Winnemucca went to Washington, D.C., to demand help from the U.S. government. She received a promise from the secretary of the interior that the Paiutes would be allowed to leave the reservation in Washington and move to Oregon. When she returned west, however, the government agent in charge of the reservation would not let the Paiutes go.

Winnemucca began giving lectures to white audiences to gain support for the Paiutes' rights. In 1883 she published her autobiography, *Life Among the Piutes*. Although Winnemucca succeeded in making the American public aware of the Paiutes' problems, at the time of her death in 1891 the Paiutes' rights still had not been restored.

Two other women who raised the awareness of Native American rights among white people were Susan and Suzette LaFlesche. Their father was an Omaha chief, and several members of their family were working to protect the rights of their people. Susan LaFlesche was the first Indian woman to become a doctor. Suzette LaFlesche was educated in private schools in the East. As well-educated women, they were able to reach many people through their lectures. Susan campaigned for better health conditions on the reservations. Suzette was most concerned with winning citizenship for Native Americans; as noncitizens they had no protection under the law. Both sisters fought against laws that forced the Indians to depend on the government for all their needs.

In the 20th century, Native Americans have succeeded in gaining certain rights, owing largely to such activists as Gertrude Simmons Bonnin. Bonnin, a Sioux, was a member of the Society of American Indians (SAI), an organization of well-educated Native Americans that lobbied for self-determination—the right of tribes to make their own decisions about their economic and political life. Bonnin wrote articles about Indians' rights to land and water use. When the SAI began to fail in 1926, she formed the National Council of American Indians and became its president.

The early 20th century was also a time of cultural revival. It was initiated in part by the growth of tourism in the United States. Tourists were interested in buying Indian baskets, pottery, and other crafts, prompting Native American women to revive traditions and skills that had been dying out.

Nampeyo, a Hopi woman, began making pottery inspired by ancient artifacts that were discovered in the 1890s. She reconstructed designs that had not been produced for centuries. The work of Nampeyo and of Maria

continued on page 62

Beverly Hungry Wolf, a Blackfoot Indian, wrote The Ways of My Grandmothers *(1980) in order to preserve the customs and legends that she learned from the older women of her tribe. The following passage demonstrates how ancient traditions have been adapted to modern life.*

A Modern Sun Dance

The way my people camp at the annual Sun Dance gathering sure has changed since the time my mother was a young girl staying with her grandparents. For instance, I don't know of anyone who still uses an open fire to cook all the meals on. And no one moves to the campgrounds with horses and wagons anymore: everyone brings their gear by truck, and a few even bring along travel trailers to stay in. There are lots of bright, orange-and-yellow camping tents, and many people use propane stoves.

When my husband and I first started camping at the Sun Dance we wanted to do it in a very traditional way. My mother helped me to sew a new tipi, and my grandmother told us to paint it in one of the two designs that she and my grandfather owned, many years ago. These tipi designs among the Blackfoot are very ancient; they get handed down from one family to the next. . . .

Even though my first tipi cover didn't take long to make with my mother's help, it was hard working with so much canvas. I marveled at the skills of my ancestors, whose tipis were often just as large, but made from big, heavy buffalo hides instead of canvas. It would have taken twelve or fourteen such hides to make a tipi like ours. Imagine lifting that many hides around in one piece! In addition, I would have had to scrape and tan all of those hides, and then I would have had to sew them all up by hand, using strips of sinew for thread. I would have had no scissors for cutting, nor needles for stitching—just my knife and a pointed awl with which to make the holes for the sinew. . . .

In the buffalo days of my grandmothers several of them got together and helped each other with their tipi-making. When one woman had all the necessary hides tanned and sinews prepared, she invited her friends and relatives for the work. She made a big meal and provided tobacco for smoke breaks. Sometimes she got an old lady to pray first and paint the faces of the workers, to ensure a well-made new home. . . .

Nowadays the women seldom even supervise anymore, much less do they put up the lodges like they used to. I always hear the men arguing over how each step should be done, and I am told that the operation went much more smoothly back when the women did it.

continued from page 59

Martinez, a Pueblo potter, inspired other Native Americans to take up traditional crafts.

Indian women were also active in preserving their languages and oral traditions. They began recording traditional songs, stories, and legends and writing their own literature in Indian languages.

Native Americans began to see some positive changes in 1924 when they were granted the right to become citizens and to vote. Their situation further improved in 1930, when the "civilization" policies were ended and tribes were given some power to make their own decisions.

However, after World War II, the government began encouraging Indians to leave the reservations and settle in cities, further alienating people from their traditions. These changes prompted more Indians to fight for self-determination. Finally, in 1975, the Indian Self-Determination Act was passed. During the next five years, government funds were given directly to tribal governments, which were allowed to decide how the money would be spent.

In the 1970s and 1980s, a number of women's organizations were formed to promote Native American culture. Their goals included preventing alcoholism, drug abuse, and family violence; improving education;

Wilma Mankiller was elected principal chief of the Cherokee Nation in 1987.

and preserving Indian languages. Indian women continue to safeguard their heritage through new schools, books, and magazines that spread knowledge of Native American culture.

Women have recently become more active in tribal leadership. In 1980 and 1981,

12 percent of the approximately 500 federally recognized tribes were led by women. In California, the state with the highest Indian population, 22 women headed tribal governments.

One extraordinary tribal leader is Wilma Mankiller, principal chief of the Cherokee Nation, the largest Indian nation in the country. Mankiller was born in Oklahoma, but her family moved to San Francisco in 1957, when Wilma was 12 years old. She became active in the Indian rights movement in the 1960s, working to secure better housing, health care, and job opportunites for Native Americans. In 1976, she returned to Oklahoma, where she continued to work in community development. She was so successful that she was elected deputy chief of the Cherokee Nation. In 1987, she ran for the office of principal chief.

Many Cherokees did not think that a woman should lead the tribe. Others reminded Mankiller's opponents that before the whites' interference, women had been important members of Cherokee government. They recalled the question that Outacitty had asked the British: "Where are your women?" Outacitty's name is interpreted to mean Mankiller. He is an ancestor of principal chief Wilma Mankiller.

Miracle, the white buffalo calf, sits beside her mother on August 31, 1994.

Wilma Mankiller discussed the return to traditional values in *Native Peoples* magazine:

> Despite the last 500 years, there is much to celebrate as we approach 1992. Our languages are still strong, ceremonies that we have been conducting since the beginning of time are still being held, our governments are surviving, and most importantly, we continue to exist as a distinct cultural group in the midst of the most powerful country in the world. Yet we must recognize that we face a daunting set of problems and issues. . . . To grapple with these problems in a positive, forward-thinking way, we are beginning to look to our own people, community and history for solutions. . . . We look forward to the next 500 years as a time of renewal and revitalization for native people throughout North America.

Native American women have in large part been responsible for the survival of their culture. They have taken on the work of reviving traditional languages, ceremonies, and myths, all helping to preserve their heritage.

One myth that has been passed down through the ages is the story of White Buffalo Woman and her promise: "I shall see you again." Through the years of turmoil, the Sioux Indians continued to hold on to the hope that the White Buffalo Woman would return to heal her people and restore harmony to the earth.

In the summer of 1994, a white female buffalo calf was born on a farm in Janesville,

Wisconsin. A white buffalo had not been seen in over a century, since buffalo herds roamed the Great Plains. The calf's birth is a sign of hope to Native Americans. Hundreds of Indians have traveled to the farm, leaving offerings of tobacco and other gifts for the calf. According to Floyd Hand, a Teton Sioux holy man from Pine Ridge, South Dakota, "She has come to bring unity, awareness and equality back to the world. This is telling us we have a chance to survive, if we pull together and save whatever is left of this Earth." ▲

GLOSSARY

adornment	increasing the beauty of an object by adding decoration
agriculture	the growing of crops; farming
anthropologist	a person who studies the cultures of other groups of people
assimilation	fitting in with a group by changing the way one acts, looks, and thinks
awestruck	filled with wonder and fear
buckskin	the skin of a male deer or antelope, used to make clothing and moccasins
culture	the customary practices and beliefs of a group of people
edible	safe to eat
embroidered	decorated with colored thread
epidemic	an outbreak of a contagious disease that affects many people in an area at the same time
fast	to go for a certain length of time without eating, for religious or health reasons
game	wild animals that are hunted
hide	the skin of an animal
influential	able to affect the actions and opinions of others
missionaries	people who spread their religion to areas where it is not practiced
nominate	to suggest a person for election to office
quills	the sharp spines that protect porcupines from other animals
sacred	holy
tan	to treat a hide in order to make leather

INDEX

ABOUT THE AUTHOR

SUZANNE CLORES holds a bachelor's degree in creative writing from Columbia University. She lives in New York City and is currently working on a collection of stories for children.

PICTURE CREDITS